TULSA CITY-COUNTY LIBRARY

PRTW
2

P9-CBZ-153

POWER CODERS

RobotRiot!

GREG ROZA

ILLUSTRATED BY JOEL GENNARI

PowerKiDS press™

New York

WT-99

Published in 2021 by The Rosen Publishing Group, Inc.
29 East 21st Street, New York, NY 10010

Copyright © 2021 by The Rosen Publishing Group, Inc.

All rights reserved. No part of this book may be reproduced in any form without permission in writing from the publisher, except by a reviewer.

First Edition

Illustrator: Joel Grennari
Interior Layout: Tanya Dellaccio
Editorial Director: Greg Roza
Coding Consultants: Caleb Stone and Kris Everson

Library of Congress Cataloging-in-Publication Data

Title: RobotRiot! / Greg Roza.
Description: New York : PowerKids Press, 2021. | Series: Power coders
Identifiers: ISBN 9781725307568 (pbk.) | ISBN 9781725307582 (library bound) | ISBN 9781725307575 (6pack)
Subjects: LCSH: Computer programmers–Juvenile fiction. | Coding theory – Juvenile fiction. | Robots–Juvenile fiction.
Classification: LCC PZ7.1.R693 Ro 202 | DDC [F]–dc23

Manufactured in the United States of America

CPSIA Compliance Information: Batch CSPK20. For Further Information contact Rosen Publishing, New York, New York at 1-800-237-9932.

CONTENTS

OH NO, WHAT'S PETER UP TO NOW?

DO YOU REALLY WANT TO KNOW?

YOU KNOW, I KINDA DO.

4

5

7

WOW! YOU BUILT A BATTLE BOT!?

THE WINNER GETS TO ATTEND A ROBOTICS SEMINAR RUN BY FIVE-TIME ROBOTRIOT CHAMP STANLEY KAPOWSKI.

CAN I DRIVE IT PLEEEEEASE!?

NO ONE WILL BE DRIVING IT.

IT DOESN'T WORK!

I GIVE UP!

EVAN MAKES SOME AWESOME ROBOTS.

BUT THE COMPETITION RULES REQUIRE THAT ALL THE ROBOTS USE AN ARDUINO MICROCONTROLLER.

THAT'S NOT GOING SO GREAT.

8

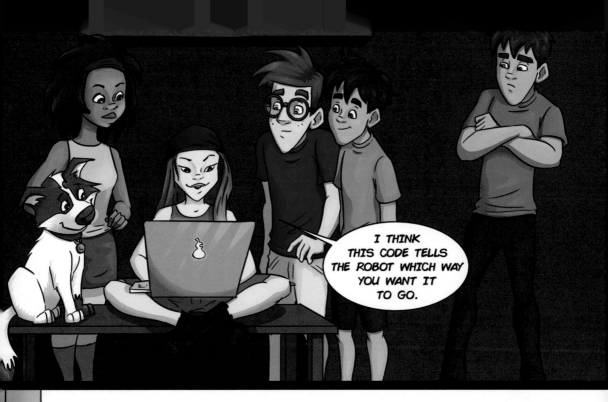

```
VOID FORWARD()
{
  SERVOLEFT.WRITE(0);
  SERVORIGHT.WRITE(180);
}

VOID REVERSE()
{
  SERVOLEFT.WRITE(180);
  SERVORIGHT.WRITE(0);
}

VOID TURNRIGHT()
{
  SERVOLEFT.WRITE(180);
  SERVORIGHT.WRITE(180);
}

VOID TURNLEFT()
{
  SERVOLEFT.WRITE(0);
  SERVORIGHT.WRITE(0);
}

VOID STOPROBOT()
{
  SERVOLEFT.WRITE(90);
  SERVORIGHT.WRITE(90);
}
```

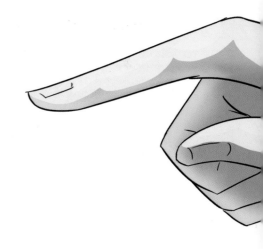

HEY, I'VE USED CODE JUST LIKE THIS WHEN PROGRAMMING LEGO ROBOTS.

SERVOS ARE MOTORS THAT CAN SENSE FEEDBACK AND ADJUST HOW THEY WORK.

THE NUMBERS HERE TELL HOW FAST EACH MOTOR IS SPINNING.

SO, 90 MEANS THE WHEELS DON'T TURN AT ALL.

THE CLOSER YOU GET TO 180, THE FASTER THE WHEELS SPIN FORWARD.

THE CLOSER YOU GET TO 0, THE FASTER THE WHEELS SPIN IN REVERSE.

BUT WAIT.

WHY DOES THE ROBOT MOVE FORWARD IF ONE WHEEL IS SPINNING FORWARD AND ONE IS SPINNING BACKWARD?

THAT'S BECAUSE THE SERVOS ARE POSITIONED OPPOSITE EACH OTHER.

RIGHT!

TO GET THEM TO SPIN IN THE SAME DIRECTION, THEY EACH NEED TO BE CODED DIFFERENTLY. AND THIS CODE LOOKS LIKE IT'S CORRECT.

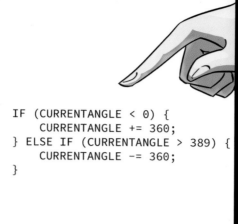

OK, THEN WHAT DOES THIS CODE DO?

```
IF (CURRENTANGLE < 0) {
    CURRENTANGLE += 360;
} ELSE IF (CURRENTANGLE > 389) {
    CURRENTANGLE -= 360;
}
```

THAT CONTROLS THE GYRO SENSOR.

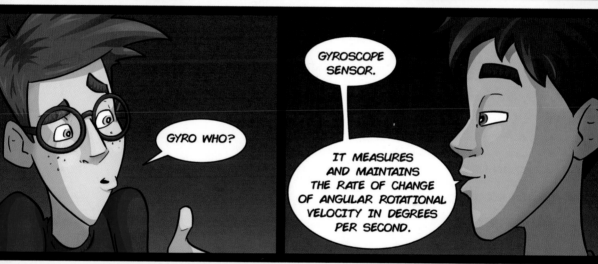

GYRO WHO?

GYROSCOPE SENSOR.

IT MEASURES AND MAINTAINS THE RATE OF CHANGE OF ANGULAR ROTATIONAL VELOCITY IN DEGREES PER SECOND.

HUH?

IT DETECTS THE SPINNING OF THE WHEELS, MEASURES HOW FAST THEY'RE TURNING, AND HELPS THE ROBOT DRIVE STRAIGHT.

HUH?

THAT'S AMAZING! I CAN'T BELIEVE YOU GOT IT TO WORK!

CRASH

WOOF!

OOPS...

```
POT1VAL = ANALOGREAD(POT1);
INPUTANGLE1 = MAP(POT1VAL, 0, 1023, 0, 179);

POT2VAL = ANALOGREAD(POT2);
INPUTANGLE2 = MAP(POT2VAL, 0, 1023, 0, 179);

POT3VAL = ANALOGREAD(POT3);
INPUTANGLE3 = MAP(POT3VAL, 0, 1023, 0, 179);
```

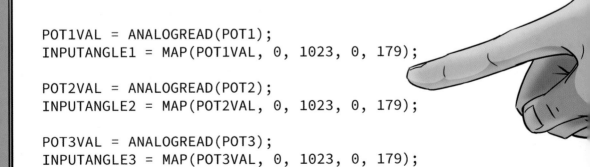

18

HEY, WAIT A MINUTE.

MAYBE THE PROBLEM ISN'T WITH THE CODE.

MAYBE THE PROBLEM IS WITH THE ROBOT ITSELF?

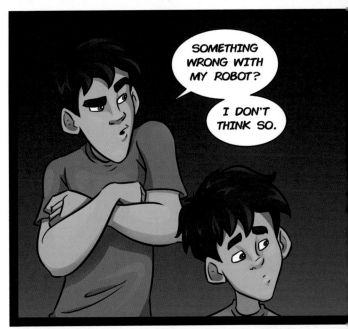

SOMETHING WRONG WITH MY ROBOT?

I DON'T THINK SO.

WELL, IT CAN'T HURT TO CHECK.

CODERS ARE CONSTANTLY DOUBLE-CHECKING THEIR WORK.

DON'T FORGET TO CHECK THE ARDUINO SETTINGS, TOO.

OH! I DIDN'T EVEN THINK OF THAT!

ABBY SET IT UP AND I JUST FIGURED SHE DID IT RIGHT.

19

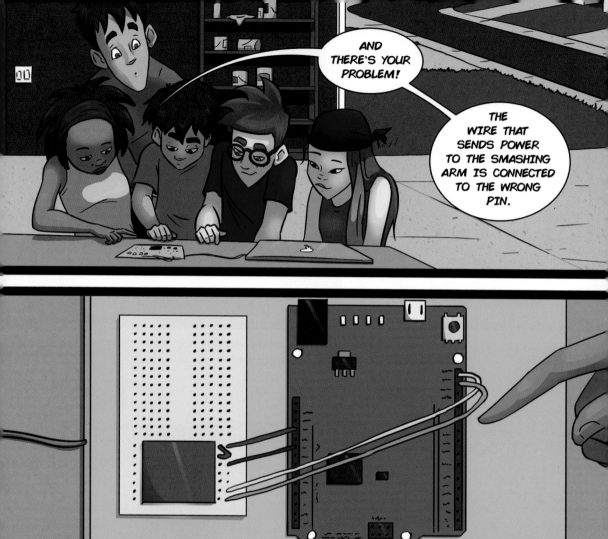

21

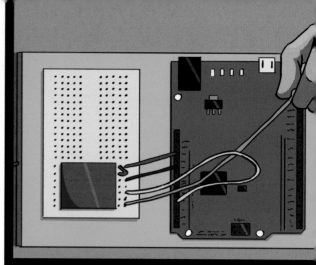

THAT SHOULD DO IT.

WHERE CAN WE TEST IT WITHOUT DESTROYING THE GARAGE?

LET'S TAKE IT AROUND BACK.

I HAVE AN OLD GARBAGE CAN THAT WE CAN TEST THE HAMMER ON.

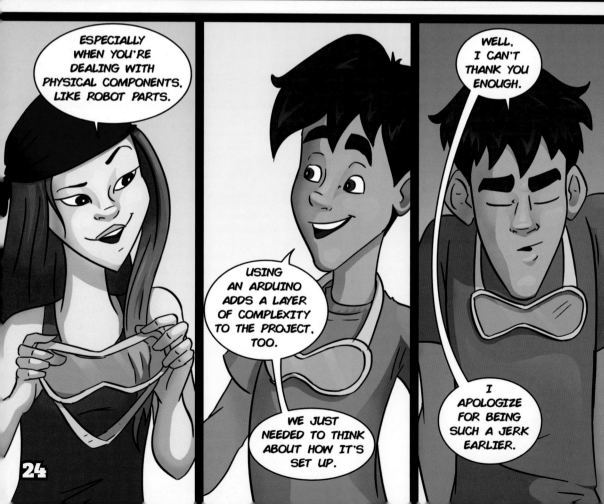

25

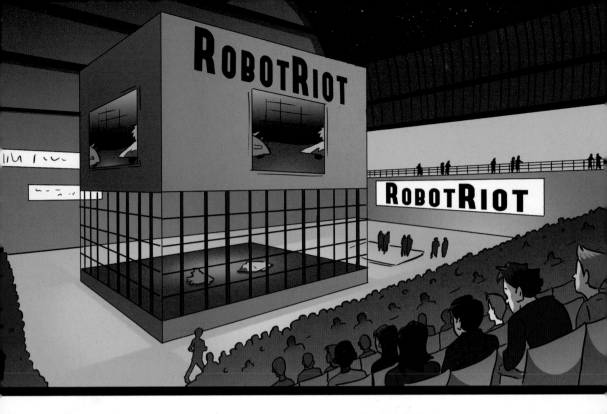